Beeny's Busy Day

Beeny the bee was resting.

"Get up sleepy head" said mom

"Good morning mom" buzzed Beeny.

"Get ready quickly Beeny. I have to go out today. So you are the one who is going to collect all the nectar" informed mom.

"Oh no! You have to go again today. I don't want to go alone. Besides, I don't know the flowers that you pick nectar from".

"Good luck my dear" said mom.

Beeny got ready and started to look for the things she needed to carry with herself.

"There it is. Mumma's honey spoon and pot. Let's do it then". And away she buzzed.

Beeny reached the forest where she knew she would be able to find the flowers who were friends with her mother.

She spotted the first flower. "Oh wow! What a beautiful colour!" she said.

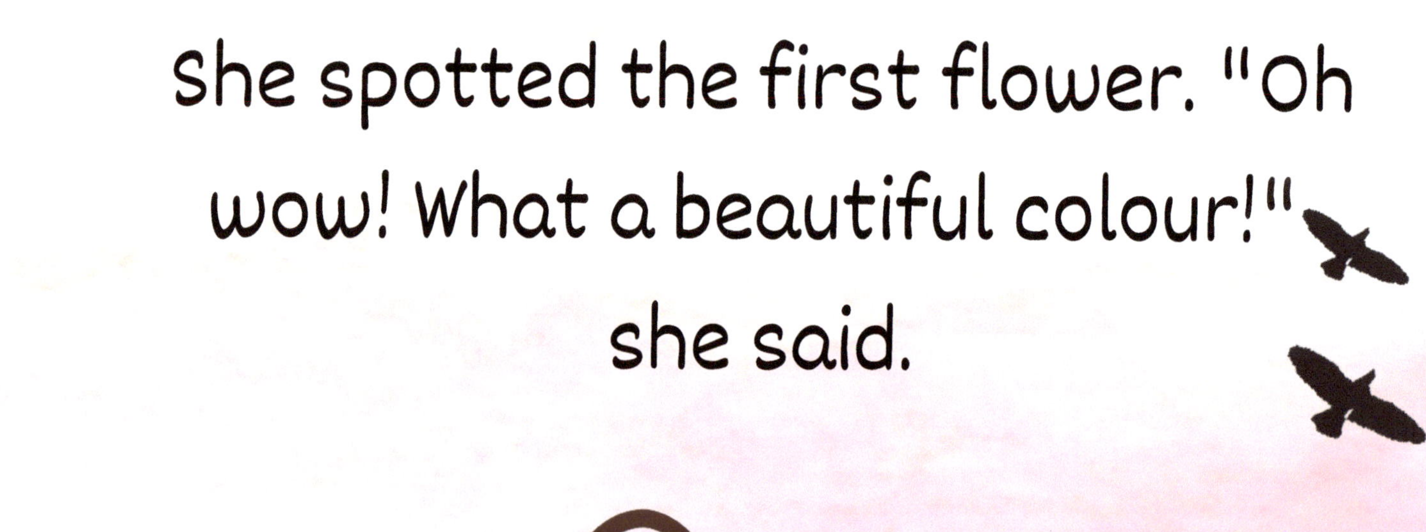

"Dear flower, what colour are you?" asked Beeny.

"I am red. How are you Beeny?"

"You know me?" Beeny was surprised.

"Oh yes! Your mom often talks about you" said red fondly.

"Can I collect nectar from you?"

"Absolutely my dear" said red.

"Thank you" said Beeny and flew ahead, carrying her pot.

"Ah! There are the other flowers" smiled Beeny happily.

"Hi" said Beeny, making herself comfortable next to the flower.

"Hi. I am blue. How are you Beeny?" replied the flower.

"Can I collect nectar from you?"

"Be my guest" said blue.

Beeny took as much as she could. Thanking blue she flew further into the forest.

As Beeny flew high, she saw some flowers down below.

"Oh my my! You are just like me" screamed Beeny in joy.

"What colour are you?" questioned Beeny

"We are yellow" said the flowers. "You are just the same colour as us", they exclaimed.

"Can I collect nectar from you?"

"Sure" said the yellow flowers. "Say hi to your mom from us" they shouted as Beeny flew away after filling her pot.

Sun was shining bright. It was mid day.

By now, Beeny was tired and wanted to rest.

She saw grass below and thought "I must rest a little now. My pot of nectar is also getting heavy" and sat down near a pretty flower.

"Who are you?" Asked Beeny.

"Can I collect nectar from you?"

"Absolutely! What is there to ask? Your mom also meets me everyday" said green.

"Thank you Green. I will see you soon" Beeny said goodbye.

Beeny's pot was almost full.

However, she still had a few flowers left to collect nectar from.

She now met Orange on her way.

"I know you" said Beeny. "My mom had got me along once and I had seen you".

"Can I collect nectar from you?"

"Yes you can little bee" said Orange.

She thanked Orange and set out to find her last flower.

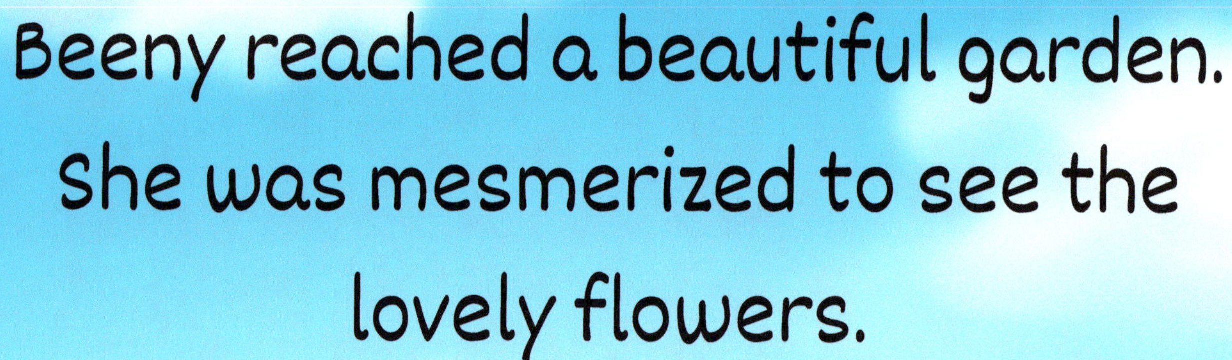

Beeny reached a beautiful garden. She was mesmerized to see the lovely flowers.

"I can see white flowers. Let me ask them if they would let me collect nectar".

"Hi! White Flowers. How are you? May I Please take some nectar? My mom has sent me".

"Of course, you may!" said the white flower and held Beeny within her petals.

Beeny thanked the flower. She now wanted to go home.

BUZZZZZZZZ

Beeny was home
now, happy with
herself.

"What a great job Beeny. You did it." said mom.

Beeny smiled triumphantly.

"Come on.. let's put all the nectar you collected in the hive".

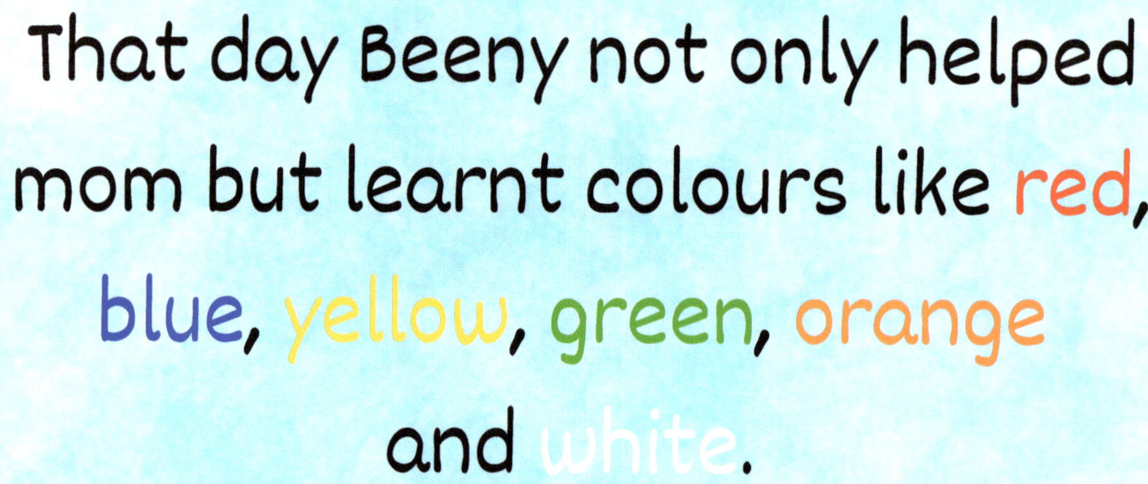

That day Beeny not only helped mom but learnt colours like red, blue, yellow, green, orange and white.

She became friends with the flowers too.

HoNey

Enjoy your honey everyday.
Its Healthy..

www.ingramcontent.com/pod-product-compliance
Lightning Source LLC
Chambersburg PA
CBHW042102110726
48006CB00002B/498

9798841176893